PERFECT PROPOSAL

TRACEY JERALD

Sarah ♡

PERFECT PROPOSAL

The proposal doesn't have to be perfect. The person asking does!

xoxo,
Tracey Garvis

Copyright © 2021 by Tracey Jerald
ISBN: 978-1-7358128-5-4 (eBook)
ISBN: 978-1-7358128-6-1 (Paperback)
Library of Congress Control Number: 2021903651

Tracey Jerald
101 Marketside Avenue, Suite 404-205
Ponte Vedra, FL, 3208

Editor: One Love Editing (http://oneloveediting.com)
Proof Edits: Holly Malgieri (https://www.facebook.com/HollysRedHotReviews/)
Cover Design by Tugboat Design (https://www.tugboatdesign.net/)
Photo Credit: Wander Aguiar
Model: Carson Twitchell

To the man who gave me the most perfect proposal.
Don't worry; I said yes.

The Midas Touch

In Greek mythology Midas, wandering one day in his garden, came across the wise satyr Silenus who was rather the worse for wear. Midas treated him kindly and returned him to his great companion, the god Dionysos.

In return for this, Dionysos granted Midas a wish. The king, not realizing the repercussions of his decision, chose to be given the magical ability to turn any object he touched into solid gold. Simple things, everyday things, Midas took for granted were instantly transformed by his touch into solid gold.

The full consequences of this gift soon became evident. At the barest touch, flowers, fruit, and water turned to gold. Midas became sick of this world he world surrounded himself with and sought to relieve himself of it.

Those finding themselves burdened with an abundance of perfection gifted to them by the gods often seek relief to reverse their fortune.

Except when that gift is love.

Prologue

CARYS

The tall, distinguished man with silver at his temples stands before me, offering his hand. "I hope you'll be happy here, Carys."

"I suspect I will be, Kristoffer. I've admired your company for a while. I've kept my eye out for the right time to make my move to become a member of it."

Kristoffer Wilde's hand tightens briefly on mine. "Really?"

"Indeed."

He tosses his head back and bellows out a laugh. "With the contract you just negotiated, I know two things about you already."

"Oh? What's that?" My head tips to the side.

"First, you're going to be an incredible asset to our legal team. Even without your impressive resume."

My lips curve upward. "Tell me the truth. Was it the intellectual property rights that caught your eye or the domestic and international distribution agreements? I know you just lost your director of business and legal affairs."

His own lips twitch. "I'll never tell. You might decide you want more money."

We share a laugh as he releases my hand. "How about I escort you down to your new office and introduce you to a few members of your team? I'm certain they'll be thrilled to stop having me breathing down their necks."

"That would be lovely."

Kristoffer comes around the desk. Just as he's about to open the door to the small conference room that connects to his New York City office, I blurt out, "What was the second thing?" At his quizzical look, I remind him, "You said there were two things you knew about me already. What's the second?"

The man standing next to me has plucked international music stars from obscurity and made them worldwide sensations. He's traveled all over the world with an ear for voices the world was meant to hear. And he has a reputation for being as honest as summer days are long.

Which is why I'm amused instead of insulted when he says, "I just know you're going to be a pain in my ass. Not only are you a lawyer, you're sharper than the tractor fender I got this scratch on." He points to a barely noticeable scar that runs near his sideburns as the door is flung open.

I slip past him murmuring, "It's my job and my pleasure to be one."

Kristoffer laughs. "Your mama and papa must be awfully proud of you."

An ache that's never quite disappeared flares around my heart. We exit the sanctum and pass Kristoffer's two personal assistants before I'm able to say, "I'm certain they would be if they were still alive."

He stops short. We're in the vestibule before solid mahogany doors—doors no one can get through without a pass from the security team just beyond them. "I'm so sorry, Carys. Human Resources lets me know if there are any red flags. They wouldn't tell me about something so personal."

"It was a while ago—almost ten years," I respond softly.

"That's why you gave up clerking for Wiltshire." He names the federal judge I'd landed an internship with when I graduated Harvard Law at the tender age of twenty-three.

"Yes. I had—have—" I correct myself. "—a younger brother. I

3

needed to be at home with him to get him through his senior year of high school and into college." I shrug as if it doesn't matter when at the time it felt like one more piece of my identity being stripped away. In one night, I lost the two people who loved me most in the world and my identity.

Everything changed.

"I might bitch about you being a pain in the ass later, but you're a good person, Carys," Kristoffer says gruffly before he opens the outer door.

My mouth falls open slightly, but I follow him quickly. I exchange the security badge I'm wearing for the visitor one I was issued downstairs. Once the two of us are tucked safely in the elevator, I've recovered enough to ask, "Tell me about the team I'll be working with."

"Don't know much about them as I try to avoid lawyers." Kristoffer shoots me a good-natured wink.

"Don't worry. I'll do my best to live down to the rest of our reputation," I inform him pertly.

He throws his head back and roars with laughter as we step off the elevator. He guides me to the right, beyond a bank of offices that line the windows, past curious stares. Finally, we reach the corner office, and he twists the handle, extending his arm inward. "Here we are."

I step past him into a dream. I move behind the enormous L-shape desk with an ergonomic office chair behind it. There's a modern printer resting on top of it, wires dangling haphazardly. I lift a brow at Kristoffer.

"Everyone in Legal has their own discreet printer. It's something our general counsel, whom I'm sure you know, badgered me into a long time ago."

"Jerry was smart to do that on several fronts." But just as I'm about to explain why, the door opens behind Kristoffer and a man backs into the room.

He's on the phone, so doesn't recognize there's other people in the room. "No, I won't be able to make it. I'm sorry. I know it's late to be canceling." There's an extended pause that goes on where Kristoffer opens his mouth to inform him of our presence.

I slice my hand in the air. This has to be one of my new employees, and I want the pleasure of being the one to handle it.

The man wraps up his call and then mutters loud enough, "It was just one date. Now she wants me to come over to meet the parents. What the hell?"

"What the hell is right," I repeat sweetly.

The man jolts in surprise. He spins around, and his face which was beginning to twist in anger fills with horror when he realizes where I'm standing and who else is in the room with me. "Mr. Wilde. Sir." Then a deferential "Ma'am. You must be the new counsel we've been hearing so many whispers about. I'm David Lennan, senior paralegal."

While I appreciate him turning a potentially awkward situation into a professional one, I don't want deferential from this man. I don't want him working for Wildcard.

Because I'm staring into the face of a god. And I just signed a document that prohibits me from doing a damn thing about it.

Fuck.

I step out from behind the desk I'd been trailing my fingers over just a few moments earlier and hold out my hand. "Carys Burke, but my colleagues call me Burke."

His eyes widen slightly. "Burke? You're Burke—the infamous lawyer who saved Zappata from paying a fine to the FCC for his on-air profanity during the Grammys?"

"It's not Z's fault the studio failed to put in their required delay. They really should have known better," I respond demurely.

He smiles as he shakes my hand, and I really wish he wouldn't. The smile is lazy and seductive, causing parts of me I was certain had fallen into a slumber to wake up with a vengeance.

Damn, I hate contracts.

I shake myself mentally before I turn to Kristoffer. "Do you mind if I have a word with Mr. Lennan?"

"Can't I stay and watch?" Kristoffer drawls.

"Kristoffer," I warn, and he holds up his hands.

"You're no fun, Carys. When you're ready, just have David escort you over to the elevator. I have a few calls to make."

As much as I want to set this too-handsome man in place for using my office to plan his trysts, I do have a job that I officially signed on to do as of a few minutes ago. Straightening to my full height, I ask, "Do you need legal representation?"

Kristoffer winks. "Not for calling my wife, though if our kids used her makeup to paint the bathroom floor again, *they* may need it to get out of being grounded."

I bring my hand up to muffle my laugh. David doesn't bother. When he laughs uproariously, he throws his head back. His neck is exposed over the tight white collar of his button-down dress shirt. Damn, I want to climb him and take a bite of it, leave my mark right where his pulse thrums steadily.

But I can't.

"Then I'll meet you downstairs in just a few moments," I tell Kristoffer.

He nods before leaving my office and closing the door behind him. The air seems to follow behind him as I find my internal temperature rising with every breath I take while I'm alone with David Lennan. Finally, I gesture to one of my guest chairs. "Take a seat."

He does, unbuttoning his suit jacket to reveal a flat stomach. The ankle of one leg comes up to rest on the knee of the other. This isn't a man who's exhibiting any great concern about being caught in his boss's office. He's calm, confident, and internally wreaking waste to my sense of calm. "So tell me, David."

"Yes?"

"Why shouldn't I rip into you for being in my office for what was obviously not a business reason?"

His lips purse. "I don't suppose the fact I didn't know you were here is a good enough excuse."

I press my hands to the desk and push to my feet until I'm looking down at him. "Not even close. I'd hate to think I can't trust one of my employees on the very day I signed the contracts to take over this division."

He slides the ankle off his knee and leans forward. Bracing his elbows on his legs, he stares up at me silently for a few moments. "You can trust me."

"Can I?" Derision slips into my voice.

"Yes. And you know why?"

"Why?" I have to force the breathlessness out of my voice as I stare down into his depthless brown eyes.

"Because, Burke, I'm going to become invaluable to you. You won't know how you worked without having me at your side." Slowly, David pushes to his feet.

I don't say anything until he makes it to the door. Then I call out. "Mr. Lennan?"

He twists his head around to face me. "We're pretty informal around here, Burke. Make it David."

I nod. "David. Let me tell *you* something."

He faces me fully. "What's that?"

"You think you're going to become invaluable? Well, I have a secret for you. So am I." I sink back into my office chair after that audacious proposition and spin around to look at the view of Rockefeller Center out my window. "Now get out of my office before I change my mind on whether or not to have your badge revoked from being able to access this office."

"Yes, ma'am." Behind me, I hear the opening and closing of the door.

I don't take a full breath for five minutes.

It's ten before I move.

And fifteen before I exit the office. Much to my chagrin, David's cubicle is right outside my door. As soon as I exit, he stands. "Are you ready to leave now, Burke?" His voice is completely polite even if there's still fire in his eyes.

I nod. Without a word between us, we head in the direction of the elevators. I'm not immune to the eyes that bore into us as we weave our way past my employees who don't know quite who I am yet.

"Thank you," I tell David politely once we reach the elevator bank.

"My pleasure." I want to call him out on his social lie, but I can't. Instead I sigh as I press the Down button.

"Burke?"

"Yes?"

He opens his mouth but shakes his head. "Nothing. It's nothing. Welcome to Wildcard." He holds out a hand.

I want to smack it, but I've spent too many years being perfect in order to reduce disruption in the lives around me. "Thank you. I look forward to working with you. With all of you," I amend.

The doors open behind me, and I slip in with a few other individuals, all who nod when I enter. Spinning around, I expect to find empty space where David was. Only it's not.

He's still there, staring right at me.

Energy arcs between us until the doors close, and I'm whisked down to the first floor where Kristoffer is impatiently waiting. With a sigh, I remove my visitor badge, knowing Monday it will be replaced with one signaling my employment.

And the perfect man I just met will be permanently out of reach.

ONE

David
<hr />

New York City pulses with an energy unlike anyplace else I've ever experienced. Since I moved here, I've fed off it. It's a thrum of electricity that hums through my system from the moment I step outside the door of the Upper West Side condo I'm fortunate enough to live in until the moment I finally close my eyes with the one person I can't live without in this world cradled at my side. Swinging my leather satchel-like briefcase over my shoulder, I begin enjoying the fourteen-minute walk from our condo on Seventy-Fourth Street to the New York offices of LLF LLC, despite the cold that's descended on the city like an arctic blanket in the last several days.

And I don't just mean the weather. Frowning, I tuck my head down and plod amid other commuters to get to work on time.

Three years ago, when working for Wildcard Music, I never would have thought my career would have taken such a drastic turn when the lawyer I worked for resigned from the music giant. I mean, this is the label that signed groups like Small Town Nights and Brendan Blake. Tightening my cashmere scarf to ward off the cold, I remember asking, "Why leave?"

My boss's response froze me in place. "The question you should be asking me is whether or not you want to come with me."

Tingles of awareness crawled up the back of my neck as if Burke's nails had just scored my neck. I swallowed with some difficulty. "Do you want me to?" I finally managed to get out.

With a negligent shrug, as if it ultimately didn't matter what I decided, Burke dismissed me by turning back to a contract on the desk. "You have two weeks to decide, otherwise I'll need to post the position to someone else."

Even though I kept doing the job I was hired to do for Wildcard and Burke, I was a seething cauldron of emotion. As a senior paralegal with a specialty in rights and clearances, I knew I had a commodity that was difficulty to replicate in my chosen field. I graduated from UCLA with a dual degree in cinematography and fine arts and held a master's degree in legal studies from Perdue. The more I thought about it, the more infuriated by it I became.

Turning the corner, I walk down toward our offices near Rockefeller Center. It was late one night, two weeks later three years ago, when we were working on a new deal for Elfinie Bischoff that my temper boiled over. Fortunately, we were the last two in our division working when I exploded and set off a chain of events that led to our now.

Incensed, I yelled, "I drafted sections of those damn contracts, Burke."

All I got in return was an arch of her perfectly curved brow and a twitch of amused lips. "And?"

"And, I think it's high time you show me some damn appreciation for what I do for you other than a pat on the back," I demanded hotly. "I deserve some recognition."

Slowly, she nodded. "I understand."

"Well then?"

"Meet me downstairs for dinner in thirty minutes. We'll discuss it then. Right now, I have to finish this contract before they're ready to finish my exit interview and escort me from the building."

Like a slap across the face, I realized it was Burke's last day and no one did a damn thing to show their appreciation.

Not even me.

Feeling selfish and foolish, I started to turn away when Burke's voice calling out my name stopped me. "Yes?" I answered.

"Maybe I never said it enough, showed it enough, but I couldn't do this without you."

Such simple words, and they meant everything to me. "Can I turn back the clock on the last few weeks?" I asked quietly.

My heart shriveled in my chest when she said quietly, "No, but you can meet me downstairs for dinner if you don't already have plans. Then we'll talk."

The breeze between the skyscrapers picks up, lifting the ends of my scarf off my coat. Turning the corner, I spy the building that houses our office near Rockefeller Plaza. Picking up my pace, I remember the nervous anxiety pulsing through me as I paced the lobby until I heard the sound of footsteps on the polished marble entryway. Burke's lips were curved as one of the evening security guards walked next to her—likely telling her all about his grandkids, I think with a touch of amusement. For all she's a sharp, demanding, take-no-prisoners attorney, beneath it is a heart of pure gold that draws people in.

Like the way she's had my devotion since the day we met because that's all I could give her while I worked for her at Wildcard. I didn't know how I was going to handle not having the chance to be near her every day. It was a proverbial punch to the gut that sent bile swirling in my mouth.

As she slipped her badge over her head—the final act of her employment at Wildcard—I realized I was gutted on every molecular level. And it was made worse when I realized the tiny little sprite was carrying her own carton of personal possessions.

I approached slowly as they shook hands. As the guard departed, he called over his shoulder, "Come back to see us soon!"

"I will, Otto!" she called back before she almost rammed into my stomach with the banker's box. "Umph!"

Snatching it away, I said heatedly, "Where are you parked?"

"The garage, but you don't have to…"

"Let's go," I said brusquely. "Then you can take me to dinner."

We ended up at this incredible restaurant with the most decadent desserts I'd ever tasted. I vehemently protested when I wasn't allowed to pick up the tab. But Burke merely smiled when she handed our server the billfold. "Let me do this for you, David. I was never able to before. Company rules and whatnot."

And then I saw it.

Felt it.

Fuck, had it been there the whole time buried beneath corporate bureaucracy and HR policies? As Burke's—Carys's—delicate fingers moved to pull back, I reacted without a sense of logic. Before I could understand how, they were trapped beneath my own. "How long?" I asked quietly.

One of the things I always liked about her being my boss was the complete lack of bullshit in our relationship. And now since that barrier wasn't there, she didn't suddenly introduce games—much to my relief. "How long have I had feelings for you?"

"Yes."

"From the moment you sat down in my office and told me you were going to become invaluable. Do you remember what I said back?"

I immediately recall that first conversation that left me feeling buzzed and loopy. It's only now I'm beginning to understand why. "You said, 'I have a secret for you. So am I.'" I blinked. "Then you turned away, throwing me out of your office."

Burke hummed. "It was that or lose my new position on the first day."

"That was two damn years ago!" I semi-roared. "You mean to tell me…"

"That I had goals, a timeline, and you weren't ready for what I wanted." A level look laid upon me let me know Carys wasn't oblivious to my after-hour proclivities. "Because let me assure you, David, the moment you enter my bed, you're not leaving it."

Sliding out of the booth, her jacket caught on the edge of the booth, pulling back away from a pair of perfectly tailored dress slacks that cupped a remarkable ass. I've always been an ass man, and the one in front of me was spectacular. I stood until I was able to reach out and trail a smooth finger down flawless skin from the corner of her brow to the throbbing pulse fluttering where short whips of hair settled next to an ear. "What do we do now?"

With a smirk, she slipped on her overcoat. "Come find me. Then we'll talk terms."

Baffled, I demanded, "We're going to negotiate?"

"Why not? We both do it so well." And on that note, I found myself watching everything, and nothing, walk away.

———

It took me less than a week of a lifeless work environment to realize my work—no, my life—just wasn't the same without Burke. Three days later, I made my way, hat in hand, to Burke's new office and was offered the job of a lifetime but under one critical condition.

"Here, I call the shots." Burke's voice was calm. She wasn't Carys—which is what I'd started calling her in my mind as I thought about her in my bed. In her new office, this unfamiliar territory, she was still Burke.

And a part of me was relieved by it.

She continued. "In this office, I'm still the boss. I've worked too damn hard and waited too long for whatever this might be to affect it."

"On one condition," I agreed.

Lips quirked. "Let's hear it."

"When you're not my boss, you're my lover. And that's where I get control."

Aqua-colored eyes lit with interest. "I can work with that."

"So can I." With a wicked smile, I leaned across the desk and asked, "Do we seal the deal with a handshake or a kiss."

"Both," Burke said, surprising me. "But lots of paperwork before we do either."

And so, it began. And for the last three years, it's worked beautifully.

Until now.

Pushing through the revolving door, I swallow the mild nausea that's been threatening when I think of what Carys is going to say when we get home tonight. I've been making significant plans that are going to forever alter the balance of our relationship.

As I stand amid the crowd of individuals waiting to crowd on the gilded elevators to carry them to the higher floors of the magnificent skyscraper to get through another workday, I wonder if any of their thoughts are as tumultuous as mine are—that nothing will be the same tomorrow as it is at this very moment.

TWO

Carys

I hear David call out a greeting to Angie as he makes his way into the outside office. My heart begins to pound when I remember the deliciously controlled way he took me up against our headboard last night. Despite the warm air allowing me to shed my suit jacket, chills run over me, raising the hair on the back of my neck.

It's been like this since I met him half a decade before. Whereas I spent a career building a reputation as a cutthroat attorney, I wanted—no, needed—David to see me as someone beyond that.

For almost two years, I tried to bury the urges he stirred in me every time he was in my presence, which was too damn often to name. Client after client, meeting after meeting, unable to do a damn thing because I was his boss, yet being forced to endure overhearing the occasional office rumors and wanting to rip someone's perfectly coiffed hair out of their head out of sheer fucking jealousy.

I'm no damn martyr, nor am I a saint. Watching David burn through relationships and my own need to be held born from assuming too much responsibility pushed me for a time into the arms of a carelessly amusing man where, fortunately, we parted amicably, realizing we were better friends. We continued to be each other's escorts when life required it. And for a short time, I was content.

The status quo changed when I came to work one day to be the recipient of David's snide remarks as he slapped a tabloid on my desk. "He's who you want, Burke?"

Lifting the paper up, I admired the photo of Becks wrapped around the lead singer of the group we'd signed the week before, Silverthorn. They made an attractive couple, my mind whirling on how I could help marketing capitalize on the PR.

"Burke!" he snapped.

With a sigh, I dropped the paper. "What do you expect me to say?"

"That you have more respect for yourself than to waste yourself on a man like that." David flicked his hand toward the paper, but, God. He could have been talking about himself.

And like the clicks of a tumbler releasing a lock, the door of my imagination flung open, showing me the path of what I needed to do.

I needed to leave Wildcard. I would never find my happiness if I saw David in this toxic environment every single day.

"You're right." I must have shocked him, because he fell back a step. "Now, if you'll excuse me?" I gestured toward the door.

"Burke?" His voice was hesitant.

"I need to make some calls, David," I told him firmly. Already lifting the receiver on my desk, I raised my brow as he stood there. "Please close the door behind you."

David cursed as he closed the door. I finished dialing, calling one of my closest friends to read over my contract to review my noncompete clause. Finding out my interpretation of it was accurate, I thanked him before hanging up.

I told the owner that evening, after dodging David with a closed door that day.

I was asked, *begged*, to stay on. Despite the offer they tempted me with, I refused. It wasn't money. As challenging as the job was, it didn't allow me the one thing I needed.

Freedom. And I got it.

A few weeks later, I called David into my office to announce my departure. He looked like I'd slapped him after I announced I was leaving. But what I didn't expect was that we'd be at odds. I thought it would tear down the walls between us.

I thought I'd made a grave mistake. That is, until his anger catapulted him into my office to demand credit and respect, when he's always had both from me, further reinforcing my decision to leave.

My life, held dormant for too long under responsibilities I inherited, flew back through my soul when his face slackened in shock seeing me being escorted out that final night. That was three years and three weeks ago today.

And I do believe it was in that moment, David ever saw *me*, not his boss. But later, when weeks after our first official date, he pulled me around the corner and angled his dark-blond head downward for our first kiss, muttering, "Don't let this be a mistake," I knew I meant as much to him as he did to me.

Now, as I type furiously on a contract template to adjust the terms for this crazy all-women metal band, I smile fondly in remembrance of the way he prowled into the office a few weeks later after that kiss carrying a slice of dark chocolate cake with dark chocolate sour cream frosting that tasted like sin bursting on my tongue, his jealousy making his eyes look more green than brown that day. And it was even more decadent when mixed with the taste of his cock as he thrust himself over and over in my mouth, kneeling astride my shoulders as I lay back on the plush office rug. But even now, I can't recall a better taste than his lips capturing mine, which were still smeared with chocolate and cum, when he thrust inside me for the first time, whispering, "You're mine."

"Damn caveman." But I can't help the curve of my lips when I remember how I writhed in his arms as he held my wrists prisoner and fucked his claim right here in this office mere hours after my ex became my client. A soft laugh bubbles out of me just as my door swings open. Though, the sight of my man causes all laughter to evaporate when I remember how irritated I am with him.

Today of all days.

"Something amusing?" He strolls across the room.

"No." At least not yet, I think to myself. Maybe by day's end.

"You were laughing when you've been in a snit. You've been like this for a while. What did I do?"

"Nothing." No, it's more like, *it's what I know you're planning on doing.* Just thinking about it sets my blood on fire. Because as much as I love the man in front of me, I want to throttle him. I have little tolerance for macho bullshit. I want a partner, someone to share their life with me.

And hearing secondhand about what David has planned makes me want to kick him hard between the legs.

"Except he'd be out of commission," I mutter aloud.

"What did you say?"

Shaking my head, I gesture to the cabinet which hides my prized Italian coffee maker. "It's out of commission. Out of beans," I tack on.

David laughs. Despite my urge to wrap my hands around his shoulders and shake him, he leans across the desk and slips his hand over mine. "You're booked solid today. I have a few before I was planning on diving into the files you left on my desk. I'll go get you a latte from Dean & DeLuca until Angie can run out at lunch for beans."

My heart defrosts a little. "You spoil me."

His face darkens before he pulls back. "Never enough. Give me a few and I'll get you sorted out for the day." With a wink he turns, saying over his shoulder, "You'll lose all your clients if you're not properly caffeinated."

I wait until David is out of earshot before I bang my head on the gel wrist pad in front of my keyboard. "Stupid man. I just need you to love me enough to stay," I whisper.

Knowing everything I do about what David has planned and realizing he's idiotic enough to let masculine-riddled convention take over his incredibly brilliant mind and fill it with debasing crap that a man needs to be the provider for his family confirms that what I have planned for today is critical to the long-term success of our relationship.

"We are who we are, my love," I whisper fiercely.

I want to race to the door and just cut loose, screaming we've evolved from prehistoric cavepeople. It's our relationship, not the world's. If we're happy, then who the hell cares what outsiders think? But this way, I think smugly, will be so much better.

Then I snap back in my chair. "He's so worried, he forgot to wish me a happy Valentine's Day," I say aloud. Bursting into gales of laughter, I wonder if I can sneak in a quick espresso before David comes back with the coffee I don't need.

And before his first gift arrives.

THREE

David
_____

"Do you have a secret to share?" I read aloud on the card that accompanies wine-colored roses delivered by courier to Burke's office. Narrowing my eyes, I cast them toward the closed door behind which negotiations for the newest metal band to hit the music scene since Mastodon are occurring. "Likely one of the people who want to know about who Burke's writing the contract for. Not like it's the first time." I shake my head and toss the card to the desk, knowing there will be nothing but a disdainful curl of a full upper lip once it's seen.

But later, much later. Because our schedule today is a block after block of blue with absolutely no wiggle room. Pulling up Burke's schedule next to my own, all I see are back-to-back conference calls from now until the day ends at seven thirty. Groaning, hating how that delays my own plans for the night, I flop back in my chair in the outer office. There's no way I can walk in there to deliver a bunch of roses, no matter how beautiful they are. "Should have thought of something like this myself," I mutter aloud. It might have made tonight's news a bit easier to swallow.

"Did you say something, David?" Her slim hand smooths over my shoulder.

"Shit." I shoot to my feet, my chair flying to one side.

Carys's aqua-colored eyes are almost amused. She makes a tsking sound. "Such language. What would a client think if they walked in?"

Since Carys Burke has a talent for melting the hearts of the scariest bad boys of rock who have walked through her door for legal advice, I just smirk. "Probably that I'm a choirboy."

Her golden eyebrows wing upward before she leans into me and presses her breasts into my back before whispering, "Well, we both know better than that, don't we?"

My mouth falls open. It must be because it's Valentine's Day because Carys is never this forward in the office during work hours. Ever. Since that wild night on her office floor when I gave in to my base Neanderthal tendencies, I've tried to be as circumspect as possible. Otherwise, I'd have her against every flat surface every chance I got, the wild attraction that started between us three years ago getting stronger with every minute of every day. But here, she's the boss, and I remain her most trusted employee. It's a relationship that's worked for us until I realized I wanted to give her everything.

But, after tonight? I don't know what's going to happen, and it's churning my stomach every time she steps out of her inner sanctum. I straighten my chair and fall back into it, moving her back slightly.

"Oh, what beautiful roses." She admires the flowers on my desk. Leaning forward, she buries her nose in the fragrant blooms, but the only thing I can smell is her. After all, I know where she dabbed her perfume this morning—just a touch behind each ear, behind her knees, and right over each pelvic bone.

But that's not it.

My heart thumps madly against my chest when she shifts and I realize what I'm smelling is her scent, that tantalizing smell I'm normally blessed with when I lay her back on our bed and I'm pushing my head between her trim thighs. Carys is immensely turned on.

I press slightly closer to her luscious ass as she leans over for the card I casually discarded before. "What makes you so sure these are for me?" Her eyes pin me to my seat as they narrow on me in contemplation. "Hmm?"

I clear my throat. Right. Work time. "I assumed they had to do with someone honing in about Erzulie deciding to use you as representation."

Much as I, myself, did, Carys flicks the card from her hand. "If you think so."

Perplexed, I wonder aloud, "What else could it be?"

"I don't know, David. You tell me. Is there anything else I need to know about?"

Now, that's a question that will get you in trouble with any lawyer. Knowing I'm dealing with my boss and not my lover, I answer honestly, "Not that I'm aware of."

Luckily, the phone rings, interrupting us. "Carys Burke," I answer. I can't prevent the curl of my lip when Carys's ex-boyfriend —who happens to be one of her biggest clients—interrupts our conversation.

"Hey, Dave. It's Becks. Is Carrie there?"

"I'll see if she has time." Knowing she'll take the call for the moneymaking asshole, I school my features before advising her, "Beckett Miller is on line one. Would you like for me to have him call back since you have a call in ten minutes with the Neo Casting Agency?"

She's already shaking her head. "I'll take it in my office. Wait two minutes after I go back in before transferring it. But for all that's holy, interrupt the call when Neo calls? I'm not blowing that over Becks's temper tantrum over finding out his latest piece is on the cover of the tabloids with another man."

"Of course." But I can't prevent the smirk as she sashays back into her office.

"And do something about those flowers, David." My head whips arounds. "Find out who sent them. That person deserves a personal thank-you."

What. The. Fuck? "Absolutely," I growl.

And it's moments like this when I'm damn glad I've made the

decisions I have because the door closing behind her tells me she's back in full-on boss mode.

Glaring at my computer, I realize I have six hours until this day ends and Carys and I can go home to make some very hard decisions.

FOUR

David

_____

"Secrets aren't a good thing," I read aloud on another dozen roses, these ones blush pink with a bright pink rim, delivered by a different courier two hours later. I spent almost that whole time trying to find out from the first florist who ordered the beautiful blooms with absolutely no luck.

"I'm sorry, sir," the store owner said snootily. "For privacy reasons, no, I can't give you a description of *any* individual who ordered from us. You said you work for an attorney? I'm certain they can advise you of that." Right before they hung up.

I was only mildly irritated before. Now, with a second delivery, I'm beginning to panic. "Son of a bitch," I curse. Did Carys pick up some kind of crazed stalker at one of the clubs? Some of the places we go to in order to check out our new clients aren't exactly in the best parts of the tristate area. Scrubbing my hands over my shaved head, I wonder, "Maybe the guy who wouldn't leave her alone at that place in Fort Washington…"

"What are you meandering about, David?" Carys's impatient voice comes from behind me.

"You got another delivery," I tell her somberly. Handing over the card, she scans it, before tossing the card onto the desk almost exactly next to the other.

"I can't think about this right now. Did you finish the preliminary contract for Erzulie?"

I push to my feet and walk to the cabinet housing our discreet printer. "Everything's right here."

"Excellent." She begins flipping through the papers quickly. "Their agent is dropping by for a draft this afternoon. I want to be able to bring them in to finalize the signing this week."

"That should work." Then I stiffen. "This week?"

"Yes. Why?"

"You're booked solid all week."

"Well, can't we move anything around?" she snaps. "Erzulie decided to go with us as her attorney of record despite the full package being offered from her recording labels. This is an enormous deal for us."

"I'm well aware of that, *Burke*." I place an emphasis on her last name as I lose my grip on my own temper. "But first, I'm not your damn assistant, Angie is. And second, even if I were, which of the other five major deals that you booked this week would you like to push back? Because according to you, they're all important!" By the time I'm done, I'm breathing hard.

Her aqua eyes turn into shards of ice. But before she can open her mouth to retort, I keep going. "Maybe this isn't quite working out the way we expected it to, Carys." I try for gentle, but she recoils as if I'd just slapped her.

"What? Us?"

"No!" I rush to get out. "Car, that's not what I'm saying at all!" I move to touch her, but she holds up a hand.

"I apologize if I've been stepping over the bounds of your work responsibilities. I'll call Angie in to figure things out."

"Carys," I start, but she simply turns around on her stiletto heel and heads back into her office, closing the door softly behind her.

I wish she'd have slammed it because then I would have felt better and not so damn guilty about having what amounts to a nervous breakdown over what I'm about to do on our anniversary combined with this crazed worry about wondering if Carys has a stalker.

Moving back to my desk, I pick up the phone to call the second florist. "Hello. My name is David Lennan. An order was just delivered with no signature on the card. Is there any way to find out who sent it?"

Just as the person starts talking, Angie opens the door to the office between us. Walking by with her tablet in her hand, she tosses me a sympathetic smile before she goes to take care of the woman I love.

Which is something I've been struggling with doing.

———

AN HOUR LATER, I RECEIVE AN EMAIL FROM ANGIE.

David,

Updated schedule for Burke.

Happy Valentine's Day!

Angie

Mentally groaning, knowing this could mean things that trickle down to me that involve contract revisions to signing new talent, it takes me a minute to understand what I'm looking at.

There are sections of Carys's schedule which are now marked off as **PRIVATE**. There's a lock in the corner that does absolutely nothing when I double-click on the meeting to open it. Are these actual meetings that I need to know about, or is this something else? A ball begins to form in the pit of my stomach as I recall the expression on her face after I yelled at her earlier.

Hearing Carys's door open behind me, I close out of the app in time for her to say, "I can't thank you enough for coming by, Ward." The two step out of Carys's office arm in arm. Whereas Carys is blonde and tiny, her brother is tall and dark. If I hadn't seen hundreds of pictures of their parents over the years, I never would have pegged them for siblings.

"My pleasure. I think things are going to work out beautifully."

She beams up at him. "I hope so. It will certainly be a change, that's for damn sure." They both laugh.

"How about I take you to lunch? You have to be starving," he cajoles her.

Carys shakes her head. "No can do, today, honey. I'm too busy."

He runs a finger along her cheek and whispers, "I got a secret for you."

She leans back. "I bet mine's bigger."

"Not for much longer." They both laugh hysterically as if they've told each other the funniest joke in the world. "Enjoy your Valentine's Day, sweetheart."

She gives a noncommittal sound as she watches her brother leave with a wry twist of her lips.

I cough. Loudly.

Carys swivels her head. "Yes?" Her voice is just a shade above arctic.

Crap. This is absolutely not how I want this day to be going. Standing, I approach her warily. "We normally don't do this during work hours…"

"Do what?"

"Us. You. Me," I state baldly. "But what I need to do can't wait until we get home later."

She sucks in a breath so huge, I can actually see it. "All right."

I swallow hard. "I'm sorry. I love you, Car."

She doesn't say anything. My stomach is lodged somewhere in my throat as I hold my breath in anticipation. Finally, she demands, "Is that it?"

Confused, and now adding hurt to my previous pissed off, I nod.

Carys stomps her foot. She actually does it twice. "I love you too, damnit. Love is not the problem here. We have other issues!" Whirling away, she goes back into her office.

This time, she *does* slam the door.

"What issues? What the hell am I missing?" Racing back to my desk, I begin poring over every piece of documentation I can from quarterly reports to contracts, trying to determine where the issues lie. What is causing her such stress? Such anxiety?

And then a knock occurs from the outer door.

Angie walks in with another bouquet of flowers. "David…" she says, hesitantly.

"Are you kidding me right now?" I demand hotly. Stalking over, I snag them out of her hands.

"Um, maybe I should keep those out here until you're ready…"

"Someone might be threatening the woman I love!" I shout my unfounded fears at Carys's receptionist. I shake the gorgeous ivory roses at her. "Some lunatic is sending flowers anonymously. I can't figure out who it is. It's likely a psycho stalker from some crazed *Dateline* episode!"

"Um, David…" Angie begins, but I cut her off.

Pacing back and forth, I cradle the bouquet in the crook of my arm. "All day, I've been panicking about asking her to marry me. I have dinner being catered—an exact replica of the Italian restaurant we went to near Broadway after she signed BBLES on as a client. It was our first date, the first night we kissed, three weeks after I got my head out of my ass after years of having her near and not managing it. Years wasted. I've wasted enough time. Tonight was supposed to be the night, and some fuckwit is messing with my plans."

"David." Angie's voice is trembling.

"For weeks, I've been planning this. Every single moment has to be perfect. She's everything, Angie, and for the rest of my life, I need to stand by her side. Is that too much to ask?"

"No, but David…" I don't let Angie finish.

"And now? Now, I can't even figure out who the hell is sending flowers so I can reassure her it's not some crazed crackpot. I'm snapping at her, hurting her, and pissing her off."

A cool voice comes from behind me, freezing me in place. "Well, since you also suck at figuring things out, I also imagine years from now our children will be coming to me for homework help." I spin around to find Carys leaning against the door, her arms crossed over her chest. "Angie, thank you for arranging David's flower delivery today."

"You're welcome, Carys. Do you need anything else, or am I good to head home?"

I stand there frozen as Carys calmly dismisses her assistant for the day. "You're fine to leave. Happy Valentine's Day to you. Enjoy your evening."

Angie can't quite keep the chortle in. "I hope you do as well. I'm sure it will be quite...memorable."

"Hmm. We shall... David!" Carys screeches as I slam the door in Angie's laughing face. For good measure, I flick the lock. "That was rude!" But the sparkle in Carys's voice betrays her humor.

"Do you realize how long I've been planning this?" I ask her quietly. I don't turn around just yet. If I do, I don't know what will happen.

"I'd say at least a month longer than I've been in talks with Ward about becoming a partner in the business, perhaps? After all"—her voice hardens—"isn't that why you approached him about a job?" My shock holds me frozen. Carys has no such problem and continues. "Tell me, David, when were you planning on giving me your resignation—before or after I said yes?"

Shit. My head thunks forward against the door. I crush the flowers in my arms and am poked with a card in the arm. I don't say anything as I hear the swish of her silk-encased legs approach me.

"Open the card," she whispers, her voice right behind my shoulder.

Reaching down, I grab the card nestled amid the bouquet of flowers. Pushing off the door a bit, I lower my head to read it aloud. "No more secrets."

"That's right. No more secrets. Now, turn around and tell me what the hell you want," she demands.

A surge of love, lust, and fury rage through me as I spin to face the pint-sized sprite with a spirit as big as a giant. Flinging the flowers to the side, I stalk forward until our bodies are touching. "First, I want to know why you were sending me roses all day today? If you were pissed, why not just ask me about it."

A beautiful smile crosses her face. "We're busy, and with Ward coming on, we're going to have so much more work to do. So, I decided we should get married soon. There's a lot to be done. With all of the appointments I asked her to fit in, Angie just couldn't manage a visit to the florist. So, I decided to send you roses. Based on your reaction, I've decided to go with the wine-colored ones. You seemed to like those the best," she concludes smugly.

"So, you're saying you were playing me, making decisions we should be making together?" I accuse.

"You're damn right I was. Exactly how you were doing that to me. And before you get pissed, tell me how it feels to have the shoe on the other foot?" I stand there fuming while Carys's smug smile blooms across her face. She licks her lips in anticipation before whispering, "Now, do you have a question you want to ask me?" she demands.

I advance toward her, a diabolical look on my face. I begin to undo my tie even as Carys slowly backs away from me. "Maybe," I say offhandedly. I flick the button at my collar open. Carys's small hands always have a problem with undoing that particular button when my shirts are overstarched.

"What?" Her voice comes out as high-pitched and screechy as Sir Walter Alfingham's did when he was dumped on the red carpet during the Grammys last year.

Her back hits the wall just as I shrug off my jacket. "We have a few things to settle first."

Her legs part as mine slips in between them. I can feel the damp heat of her pussy against the thin wool of my suit trousers. She breathlessly pants. "Like what?"

"Like this." And pinning her hands to her sides, I lower my head and capture her lips.

FIVE

Carys

Even as David backs me against the wall, I can tell he's warring between the need to fuck me or kill me.

Too damn bad. If he wanted his perfect Valentine's Day proposal, he shouldn't have gone out job hunting, to my brother of all people. I damn well know what he was trying to do—level some stupid, testosterone-laden playing field between us.

"Didn't think I would find out?" I say sweetly as he approaches, his long legs eating up the distance between us as I remember the phone call from over a month ago that has set me on a knife's edge since alternately hoping he'd pull his head out of his ass and talk with me and hoping he do exactly what he's doing right now so I can have the pleasure of yanking it out with both of my own hands.

"In case you're wondering, I gave you the referral that Ward called for," I taunt.

David growls. "Remind me to thank Ward later." His hands slap on either side of my head, trapping me against the wall.

But just bringing up David's obtuse behavior sets off my own temper. I place my hands into the center of his rock-hard chest and push. He doesn't budge.

I let out a growl of my own, much like I did when I hung up the phone with Ward that day.

"I didn't think a referral would be a problem," Ward said laconically in response to my complete silence on the other end of the line.

"Oh?" I was immensely proud of myself for not allowing the betrayal to slide into my voice. Only to have it erased my utter shock when Ward howled with laughter in my ear.

"I don't know how the two of you have managed to work alongside each other and still build what you have, Carys," he says wistfully. "But if I was planning on marrying the woman I love…"

There was no holding back my screech of "Excuse me?" at that point. Surging out of my chair, I ignored the view from my office as I began to pace agitatedly.

Ward muttered, "Shit. Did I let the cat out of the bag?"

"More like you dumped the ring out of the box," I flung back hotly. "Now, spill it, Ward. You're my damn brother, for Christ's sake."

Reluctantly, he did, knowing it would be so much worse for him if he didn't tell me what I want to know.

I fell back into my chair, stunned. "All he had to do was say something," I whispered weakly. "From the moment we met, all I've ever wanted was David. Hell, I gave up working at Wildcard just for a chance…"

"And now it looks like he's trying to do the same thing, only you don't have a fraternization policy," my brother said gently.

"For obvious reasons," I retorted.

"The question is what are you going to do about it?"

A million thoughts ran through my head, pulling me in opposing directions, but at the center grounding me was one thing. David.

But I'm not known for thinking on my feet for nothing. A memory of an idea Ward and I had ages ago long before tragedy forced me to become my brother's guardian as well as his sister stirred back to life. I ran through the possibilities quickly, and the answer was so clear it left me as smug as a cat with a saucer full of cream.

Tipping my chair back, I said, "What would you say if I told you fine?"

Ward choked on the coffee that's never far from his reach. "That you have a screw loose. What are you thinking, Car?"

"I'm thinking you can have David." I paused for one heartbeat... Two. "But I get you in exchange."

There was silence on the other end of the line before Ward pieced it together. "You mean..."

Now, with every rise and fall of David's chest that I can feel under my hands, the incredulity in his olive-green eyes, I feel vindicated. "You were going to decide my future without consulting me?" I demand.

By the way David freezes, it finally penetrates how utterly infuriated I am. Ever since the car wreck that took my parents' lives, I've never had the luxury of being helpless. I was never able to cede control about anyone, anything, because I had duties and responsibilities too great to shirk.

I walked away from a prestigious job clerking for a federal judge to move back to New York to ensure my younger brother Ward had the stability of our family home while finishing high school and going to college. I set my life, my dreams, on hold long enough to make certain he would have every opportunity to thrive without Mom and Dad.

And then I felt like God was playing a sick joke on me the day I walked in on my dream job at Wildcard and I felt my heart be touched by angels only to be laughed at by the devil all in one breath.

"You're going to leave me," I accuse, pain evident in each word I hurl at him.

David's eyes close. "Never."

"You are," I press. "You took a job with my brother." Pain seeps out of every word.

"I thought..." He shakes his head before determination sets in.

"You thought to prove something to other people who might judge us. Judge you for working for your girlfriend? Your wife?" My voice chokes up at the end.

His mouth opens and closes several times before his head drops down against mine. His fingers tangle with mine against the wall before he admits, "You're right."

Slowly, I nod, accepting his actions for being out of love instead of malice. His apology evident in every puff of air we exchange, David leans down and presses his mouth gently against one eyebrow, then the other. One cheek, the other. The corner of each lip. And then finally, he brushes his lips across mine once, twice, until I grant him entry.

Our kiss is languid, tongues that twine our hearts tightly together mixed with the harsh, heated promise of passion. It's apologies, promises, and vows, spoken in the true language before God confounded speech through the tower of Babel. It's passion between two people who have touched each other intimately, who know down to their souls what lies beyond sex when love is involved.

We stand there, our hearts touching, our breath mingling, for long moments before David whispers, "You know how I grew up, Car. My dad's the man of the house—constantly telling me how he's the one out providing for the family, for my ma. Never fails to bring up every time we talk how he's busting his ass to make sure everyone has what they need. Here? You give and give—from a stunning home to a job. It all is because you gave it to me. Maybe I needed to know what I could do on my own," he admits, the vulnerability behind his actions clear.

And any lingering anger I have seeps away. Reaching up, I frame his face with my hands. "My love, if I have so much to give, it's because I lost so much. Please remember that."

His brow furrows, but he nods. "I know."

"Don't you know, I'd rather be struggling to pay the rent and student loans than have millions of dollars at my disposal? That Ward would too if we could bring our parents back to life?" I shake my head against his as his arms wrap around me. "The home you and I live in is theirs; we're just filling it with the love that was missing for so many years. That's what you bring to it, to me." I lay my hand over his heart. "What's in here has more value than anything. And the idea of not being with you every day? It gutted me, David. It made me think you didn't want to be with me."

"Not that. Never that, Carys," he groans.

"Okay. Now I have a question?"

He presses his lips to my forehead. "What's that?"

"Does this mean I still get to plan our wedding? I had Angie all excited about getting an extra two weeks of vacation this year for our honeymoon."

My lips part as David reaches up and renders the two sides of my red silk blouse open. Buttons scatter in every direction.

My pussy begins to get wet when I see the tight skin pulled across David's cheekbones. "Any questions?"

Holy. Shit.

"Just one," I whisper. "Please, touch me."

SIX

David
___

I lose all semblance of control when her hand touches my chest. Boosting Carys to the wall with my hips, I wrap her legs around my waist and reach down to the V of her delicate red silk blouse.

Tearing hard, buttons scatter in every direction. In the furthest recess of my mind, I hear one ping off the window with a tiny clink. I don't care. The only thing that matters is furthering the emotional and physical connection with the woman in my arms, in my heart. "Any questions?"

Rocking my hips into hers, I swell tighter as she lets out a breathy sigh. "Just one. Please, touch me."

"Control yourself, Car," I murmur as I feast on the long, elegant line of her neck.

"That's hard to do when you're…" Carys's moan rips through the air as I bite down on the tendon while pressing my thick cock against her. "Again," she demands.

I laugh darkly before I smooth a hand up the side of her leg to give it a quick pop. I'm rewarded by her ecstatic whimper. "Who's in control here, Carys?" I remind her, pulling back.

She licks her puffy lips before saying, much to my delight, "You are."

Dropping her legs, I grab her wrist and drag her over to the credenza by the window overlooking the Manhattan skyline. Laying Carys's cheek and chest down on it, I'm so fucking hard, I might split the zipper of my trousers. "Only you can make me this way," I tell her honestly.

"How?"

I push my hips against her luscious ass. Her moan fills the room and my heart to the brim.

My lips curve as my hands slide beneath the hem of her short skirt. But where I expect to find soaked panties that I fully intended on ripping off before my hand lands on her ass, I'm met with her creamy skin. "Sweetheart, what am I going to do with you?" I make a tsking sound. I bring my hand back slightly, not hard enough to hurt her—never that—when her words freeze me in place.

"Anything you want as long as we do it together forever." Tears spike her lashes, turning the gorgeous aqua color to pools of ocean water.

Suddenly, I want to be inside of her as I feel her body ripple from the inside out with each shudder. Laying myself over her, my hands quickly make work of my belt, then the fasteners, before I release my cock still trapped inside the silky boxers.

Carys moans beneath me, wiggling her ass up against my hardness.

"Shh," I soothe her, shoving the material of all of the items separating my body from hers to the floor. As I kick her legs apart with my feet, her sigh of pleasure releases a bloom of happiness inside of me. One I know will never go away no matter how many years pass, no matter how much age changes us.

Because this woman completes me by accepting me, challenging me, and giving me everything I need every day.

"I love you, Carys," I choke out.

She turns her head slightly. I let her. I want this moment, this gateway to our forever that she so cleverly figured out, to be imprinted on her soul.

Covering her delicate body, I run two fingers through swollen lips, deliberately dragging them over her extended clit. "You're drenched," I murmur.

"It was so fun waiting for you to realize it was me," she taunts, just as my hand lands on the outside of her thigh.

Her hip jerks in reaction, her thigh twitching. "Uh! Yes," she hisses.

"Do you want more?" I ask.

Her eyes lower. "Do I deserve more?"

Fuck yes, but then again, so do I. I grunt as I grab hold of the base of my dick, sliding it in between her wet folds. Lining myself up, I whisper, "You deserve everything," before I push myself in slowly, drawing out this moment for exactly what it is—the final merger of our lives into one eternity.

Leaning back, my hands roam her perfect skin, knowing it's going to pinken so perfectly. "You were made for me," I tell her.

"Yes." Her lips quiver as she answers.

I reward her with a thrust and a slap to her cheek. Her tiny foot raises, the heel catching me on the ass to tug me closer.

I thrust a few times deeply, causing us both to moan and pant, before I screw myself tightly inside. "We were meant to love each other."

"We were," she agrees.

I land a smack to the outside of her other leg. I feel the ripples of her pussy along my cock, even though I don't move. "Hold off, baby," I warn her.

She nods frantically, lifting slightly, pressing her forehead to the table.

But I want her eyes for the last part, the part that will make her mine forever. Pulling out, I ignore her cry of "No!" before I spin Carys to face me. Boosting her atop of the credenza, I step in between her legs and wrap her arms around my shoulders, before my cockhead nudges her opening.

"Be mine. Forever. Don't stop loving me, Carys. Marry me," I choke out hoarsely.

The smile that curves her lips is so incongruous with the overflow of tears. But it's the sweet "Yes, David. It would be the happiest day of my life to become Mrs. David Lennan" that has me slamming my cock inside of her over and over until Carys calls my name when she comes tightly on me, her pussy rippling all over my cock.

Burying my face in her neck, I shoot my load a few thrusts after.

Moving us from the credenza to the floor, I pull her over my chest as we both lie there panting. "I'm still pissed," I mutter as I brush her damp hair away from her forehead.

Lifting slightly back, Carys smiles. "Why?"

"I had it all planned." I sound like a petulant little boy now that I'm not controlling the one thing I need to control in our lives.

She leans forward and presses her lips against mine gently. "You planned what you thought I should have, what the world expects. Not what we need. This—" She waves a limp arm to indicate the destruction we've wreaked on the office. "—is what we needed, my love. Me knowing you're never going to walk away and…"

A light turns on. God, she's so damn brilliant on top of being the most beautiful woman I've ever met. And now, she's going to be mine. No, that's stupid. She's always been mine—since the moment I first kissed her three years ago. "And I know that no matter what, we still have balance in our lives. That money, work, doesn't define our love. Only we do that."

Carys beams at me before lowering her head down on my chest. "Exactly."

I begin to chuckle, softly at first, then full-throated roars. Carys props herself up on an elbow. "Care to share the joke?"

I manage to gasp, "I had candlelight, and…and…"

"And?"

"Violins!" I tip my head back. "I need to cancel the violins!"

Carys begins giggling. Soon, we're clutching each other, holding on to the only thing that matters during the perfect proposal—the person you love.

MUCH LATER THAT NIGHT, WE'RE BACK IN OUR CONDO. AFTER WE'VE made love before gorging ourselves on reheated Italian leftovers I had catered from Daniela Trattoria, I slide a solid white-gold-and-diamond Claddagh ring on her left hand with the heart pointed out —just like the way her father slid a similar ring on her mother's hand long ago. A ring that symbolizes everything she's worked for: life, love, and friendship. After all, she named her company after it.

Lifting her trembling fingers to my lips, I murmur, "You have my heart, my love, and my loyalty, Carys. On the anniversary of a day when I knew I'd never be the same."

"When you walked in my office the first time, I realized I never would either," she whispers.

"I wish I had recognized it sooner." I start to apologize for the eight millionth time, but she's shaking her head.

"We happened the way we were supposed to happen," she says simply.

A smile breaks out across my face. "Rather like our proposal happened the way it was supposed to happen?"

She nods emphatically. "Demanding, full of heat, and unpredictable. Exactly like we've been from the beginning."

Lowering my head to hers, I kiss her with all the wild passion she stirs in me. "In other words, perfect."

Epilogue

CARYS

"David, I'm pregnant. I'm not an invalid," I snap at my husband of six months.

"If you think I'm taking you on the floor of your office like some animal, you're crazy, baby," he fires back.

"It hasn't stopped you before!"

"You weren't eight million months pregnant."

"I'm three weeks from my due date. Nothing is going to happen except I may die from excessive need." I run my hands up my silk-encased thighs. David's eyes darken knowing I'm just wearing thigh-highs with an elastic band underneath since he had to slide them in place this morning. After all, even seeing my feet at this point feels like a memory I'm never going to regain.

But I get hot every time my husband wears that particular suit, and he knows it. It was the one he married me in, damnit.

It was a good thing we got married just a few months after David popped the question. Neither of us had a clue I was close to three months pregnant on Valentine's Day. My periods—always irregular, requiring me to be on the Pill—had stopped coming. I hadn't noticed between the stress of the holidays, David's possible defection to work for Ward, and getting engaged. It wasn't until I went wedding dress shopping at Amaryllis Bridal with Angie that I noticed a very firm knot where my body was once concave.

"Oh my God!" I shouted, causing wedding dress goddess Emily Freeman to glance up in alarm as she was clipping me into a form-fitting mermaid dress.

"Is everything okay, Carys?" her sweetly Southern voice floated between us. "I didn't pinch you, did I?"

"No. It isn't that. I… Oh, my God. I think I'm going to cry." And I sank to the floor in one of her original creations that cost more than most people's first cars.

Then I burst into tears.

Emily, calm as you please, just reached over for a box of tissues and placed it in my hand. "I remember my sisters going through the same thing each time. They were complete wrecks. Though admittedly, their husbands were worse."

My head snapped up. "You know? How? I just figured it out myself."

Emily hauled me to my feet. Taking my hand, she spun me toward the mirror. "Carys, it's written all over you: the serenity, the blooming, the joy." She placed the hand she was still holding on my lower abdomen. "If there's two people who don't know, it's likely you and your David, and that's because you're so intent on making your wedding perfect you forgot something important."

"What's that?" My voice is husky to my own ears.

"The life you have with him already is. This is just an extra gift you're giving to each other." Emily squeezed my waist where I had a new secret for David. A secret so perfect, I wondered if I could wait to tell him until I got confirmation.

Some of what I was thinking must have been on my face because Emily began to laugh. "Now, do you still want a tight-fitting mermaid?"

"Hell, no. I might not be able to zip the sucker by the time the wedding comes in two months." I didn't care what arguments David used; I was still getting the wedding I planned with Angie. My brother was still going to walk me down the aisle.

And I was still going to carry the flowers I'd sent him for Valentine's Day.

It was going to be perfect.

"Then let's get you out of this dress. I have something in mind I think you'll love." Emily quickly helped me out of the dress before disappearing for a while. When she came back in, it was with a dress —the dress. "It's a ball gown, embroidered bodice, and an embroidered cascading tiered skirt. It's…"

"I'll take it," I declared without having tried it on.

Emily grinned. "Don't you want to know its name?"

"It has a name?" I tipped my head to the side.

"All of my dresses do. This one is called 'Love's Perfect Rose.'"

Feeling tears prick my eyes over the perfect promise the dress held in so many different ways, I whispered, "Will you help me try it on?"

And once it slithered across my body, I knew it was it. Just like some part of me knew David was the man years before. "Will I be able to get it in time?" I asked the last question.

Emily had an odd smile on her face. "I went to pull the original, Carys. You're the first person to wear it. It's yours. All we have to do is the final fitting, which I suggest we do the week before the wedding."

And as Emily turned to get her tablet and I stared at myself in the mirror, I realized that for the first time since my parents' death, I wanted for nothing. I had it all.

Life was perfect.

Now, as I stand arguing about sex with my husband in our office, I grin as I waddle toward him. "Did you ever imagine it would be like this?"

He shakes his head as he reaches for me and spins me around. My stomach is protruding so much that when David wants to get close, he fits his body behind mine. But in all the ways that matter, we've become partners—by each other's side always.

It's a perfect balance of work and home life that works for us.

Even Ward has calmed down some of his wicked ways. More and more of late, I catch glimpses of my father in him. I wonder if that has to do with him finally recognizing what's been in front of him the whole time.

Only time will tell.

I'm just about to ask my husband if he's ready to walk home when there's a strange tightening across my abdomen. "They weren't kidding about the strength of those Braxton—" I don't get the rest of the sentence out as a stream of fluid begins to leak down my legs. "No, it's impossible," I whisper.

"What?" David demands. As he spins me in his arms, I'm grateful he has such a tight grip on me. "What's impossible, Carys?"

I open my mouth to answer him, but all that comes out is a low groan as a contraction snakes its way from my back across the front of my abdomen.

David pales. "No, it's too soon. We're not ready. It can't be happening now."

I begin to deep breathe, just like they taught us in Lamaze class. Once I realize there's not another contraction imminent, I reach up and cup David's chin. I tug him slightly, and he presses his forehead against mine. "Don't worry. If he's anything like his father, he's going to be perfect."

David seizes my lips in a fierce kiss. "That's after his mother shows him the most important thing."

"What's that?"

"How to love."

Later that night, I realize I didn't manage to seduce my husband in the now wrinkled suit I married him in. But looking down at the bundle wrapped up in my arms, I realized it's a certainty I'll never be able to resist him wearing it.

Ever.

Because he's now worn it to the two most special events of our lives: our marriage and the birth of our son. In other words, if I have my way, he's never getting rid of it.

I lean down and whisper into my son's ear, "I have a secret to tell you."

David grins. "Sharing secrets with our son already?" He hitches a hip on the side of my bed and presses a kiss first to the top of my head, then to our son's.

I nod before continuing. "The secret is this: love is worth everything, Benjamin Burke Lennan. Everything. And no amount of money, prestige, or fame will ever replace that."

"Listen to your mother," David chokes out.

I tip my head back, and my lips curve. "Practicing that for when he's older?"

David doesn't answer. Instead, he takes my lips in a kiss that's more than a thank-you, more than an I love you. It's exactly one thing.

Perfect.

Also by Tracey Jerald

Midas Series

Perfect Proposal

Perfect Assumption (Coming April 2021)

Perfect Composition (Coming Summer 2021)

Perfect Order (Coming Fall 2021)

Amaryllis Series

FREE - AN AMARYLLIS PREQUEL

(NEWSLETTER SUBSCRIBERS ONLY)

FREE TO DREAM

FREE TO RUN

FREE TO REJOICE

FREE TO BREATHE

FREE TO BELIEVE

FREE TO LIVE

FREE TO WISH: AN AMARYLLIS SERIES SHORT STORY - 1,001 DARK
NIGHTS SHORT STORY ANTHOLOGY WINNER

FREE TO DANCE (COMING SPRING 2021)

Glacier Adventure Series

RETURN BY AIR

RETURN BY LAND

RETURN BY SEA

Sandalones

CLOSE MATCH

RIPPLE EFFECT

Lady Boss Press Releases

CHALLENGED BY YOU

Acknowledgments

First, to my husband who made my own proposal absolutely perfect. Thank you for asking, my love!

To our amazing son. I'm terrified by the fact that by the time this book goes to print, you will actually be taller than me. You were perfect as a baby in my arms and you still are now.

To my mother, who always thought I was perfect even when I wasn't.

To my Jen. I never had to be perfect. Thank God.

To my Meows, for wanting to make me perfect on that one special day. I've never forgotten that dress.

To Sandra Depukat, from One Love Editing, for making my stories have that extra touch of something.

To Holly Malgieri, from Holly's Red Hot Reviews, a.k.a. my twin, you will find your perfect. I have no doubt!

To Deborah Bradseth, Tugboat Designs. You always seem to reach into my mind and pull out exactly what I am thinking!

To photographer Wander Aguiar, Andrey Bahia, and model Carson Twitchell, this photo was everything! Thank you all!

To Gel, at Tempting Illustrations, it hasn't been the easiest year and still you bring me beauty. Sending you all the XOXOs.

To the fantastic team at Foreword PR, thank you for everything you do! Always!

Linda Russell, I can't begin to say what you mean to me. Perfect doesn't come close to describing it. The best days, the worst days, you're there. And I'm grateful you're in my life.

To Shari Ryan, who not only saves my sanity but keeps me from going down a rabbit hole regularly.

To Susan Henn, Amy Rhodes, and Dawn Hurst, my dream team! I don't know what I would do without any of you!

For my amazing crew in Tracey's Tribe, every day is made more amazing because of you!

And to the for all of the readers and bloggers who take the time to enjoy my books, thank you.

About the Author

Tracey Jerald knew she was meant to be a writer when she would re-write the ending of books in her head when she was a young girl growing up in southern Connecticut. It wasn't long before she was typing alternate endings and extended epilogues "just for fun".

After college in Florida, where she obtained a degree in Criminal Justice, Tracey traded the world of law and order for IT. Her work for a world-wide internet startup transferred her to Northern Virginia where she met her husband in what many call their own happily ever after. They have one son.

When she's not busy with her family or writing, Tracey can be found in her home in north Florida drinking coffee, reading, training for a runDisney event, or feeding her addiction to HGTV.